The Little Snowgirl

AN OLD RUSSIAN TALE
ADAPTED AND ILLUSTRATED BY

Carolyn Croll

A WHITEBIRD BOOK
G. P. Putnam's Sons
New York

For Jane and Barney Freedman with love

Library of Congress Cataloging-in-Publication Data
Croll, Carolyn. The little snowgirl. "A Whitebird book."
Summary: Caterina and Pavel's wish for a child is fulfilled
when the snowgirl Pavel makes in the yard comes alive.
[1. Fairy tales.   2. Folklore—Soviet Union]   I. Title.
PZ8.C8686Li 1989   398.2'1'0947   [E]   88-30667
ISBN 0-399-21691-X

First impression

A long time ago in Russia lived Pavel the woodcarver and his wife, Caterina. They were not rich, but they were not poor either. They had a good house to live in, warm clothes to wear, and plenty to eat. They had been married for many years and loved each other very much, but they were sad because the one thing they wanted more than any other in the world was a child of their own.

Now it was Christmastime again and it seemed to Caterina
and Pavel that all the other cottages in the village were full
of bright-eyed girls and boys singing *kolyady*, the Christmas

carols, and trying to be good so that Babouschka would
bring them a present when she went from house to house on
Christmas Eve. This made Caterina and Pavel even sadder.

One day it snowed in the village and Caterina and Pavel
watched as the children came out to play. Pavel saw
Caterina brush away a tear as she turned to the samovar
to make the tea.

When Pavel looked out again, the children were building
a snowman. It made him smile to watch the fun.

Later that night when Caterina was fast asleep, Pavel was wide awake thinking about the children playing and how sad Caterina had been watching them. Then Pavel had an idea.

Quietly, he got out of bed, dressed, took his lantern, and stepped into the night.

Pavel began to roll and pat the snow. It was hard work
and his fingers froze, but Pavel didn't seem to notice and just
before dawn he finished.

Pavel was so excited that he could not wait to show Caterina what he had done.

"I am sorry to awaken you, my dear, but there is something that you must see," Pavel said.

Caterina rubbed her eyes, put on her shawl, and followed Pavel into the yard.

"She's not a real child, but she is ours," Pavel said.

At first Caterina was very happy, but as she looked at the
little Snowgirl, she began to feel sad again.

"If only she could speak, if only she could run and play like other children," Caterina said.

No sooner had Caterina spoken than something strange happened.

"It must be the morning light," Pavel said uncertainly.

But then they both heard the little Snowgirl laugh.

Caterina and Pavel watched her and then Caterina said, "Husband, it is freezing out here. We must bring the child into the cottage where it is warm. Come, Dochinka, little daughter."

"Please, Mother and Father, I must not go into the cottage. I am a child of snow, and I must stay where the cold wind blows," the little Snowgirl said.

"Perhaps you are hungry, Dochinka?" Caterina asked. "I will fetch you some good hot porridge."

"Thank you, dear Mother, but your porridge is too warm for me. If you would just crush some ice in a bowl, that will be my porridge," the little Snowgirl said.

The thought of such a frosty breakfast made Caterina
shiver, but she gave the little Snowgirl what she had
asked for.

Just as the little Snowgirl finished eating, the village children came out to play. The little Snowgirl ran to meet them, and they were happy to have a new friend.

Caterina and Pavel watched the children together and this time, when Pavel saw tears in Caterina's eyes, he knew that they were tears of joy.

When evening came and the village children left to go home for their suppers, Caterina said, "You must be hungry and tired from all your play, Dochinka. Come and we'll have some hot cabbage soup and make you a bed by the stove."

"Dear Mother, you are so kind, but I am a child of snow, and I must stay where the cold wind blows. So I must not eat your hot cabbage soup, and I will be happy to have my bed right here," she said.

Poor Caterina. Nothing that she or Pavel said would
change the little Snowgirl's mind. So while Pavel made the
child a soft snow bed, Caterina crushed some ice in the
wooden bowl.

The little Snowgirl ate all her icy supper, and when she had finished, Caterina and Pavel tucked her into her frozen bed and kissed her cold little cheek.

Caterina and Pavel welcomed Christmas as they never had before. They got right to work making presents for their little Snowgirl.

While Caterina baked mushroom pies and honey cakes, the little Snowgirl filled the kettle with clean new snow to melt for soup. Then she helped Pavel gather wood.

"Such a good and helpful child," Pavel said.

"If only she would sleep by the warm stove and eat *hot* porridge and cabbage soup, I wouldn't worry so," Caterina said.

On Christmas Eve Caterina set the supper on the table.

"Dear Dochinka, surely you will have a Christmas cake still warm from the oven?" Caterina asked.

But all the little Snowgirl wanted was her bowl of ice porridge.

While she ate, Pavel told her about old Babouschka.

"On Christmas Eve, when everyone is asleep, Babouschka comes carrying her candle, looking in every cottage for good and loving children so that she can give them what they wish for most in the world," Pavel said.

"So you must think what you will ask for," Caterina said with a smile.

"I have everything that I could want already," said the little Snowgirl.

But when Caterina and Pavel bent over to hug and kiss her good night, there was so much love in their faces that the little Snowgirl thought, "I know what I shall ask for."

Caterina and Pavel went to bed but Caterina could not
sleep.

"What kind of mother and father lets their little daughter
sleep in the snow, and on Christmas Eve?" Caterina said.
"Babouschka will never find her if she's not in the cottage."

"But she says that she must stay outside," Pavel said
sleepily.

"Well *we* must do what *we* must do!" Caterina whispered.

On Christmas morning Caterina and Pavel could not wait to hug their little daughter and give her their presents.

"Wake up, dearest Dochinka. Come and see what Babouschka has left."

The little Snowgirl did not stir.

"What have we done?" Caterina and Pavel cried together.

"I shall never forgive myself." Caterina wept into the small coat.

Sadly Pavel picked up the bear he had carved and made it dance on its stick.

Then suddenly they heard a soft little laugh.

Caterina and Pavel turned around and there stood their little Snowgirl, but something was different.

"Babouschka has brought me what I wanted most in the world, just as you said she would, Father. I am no more a child of snow, and I can stay by the fire's glow," sang their little daughter, and she threw her arms around them both. But this time her arms were warm.